W9-CCP-047

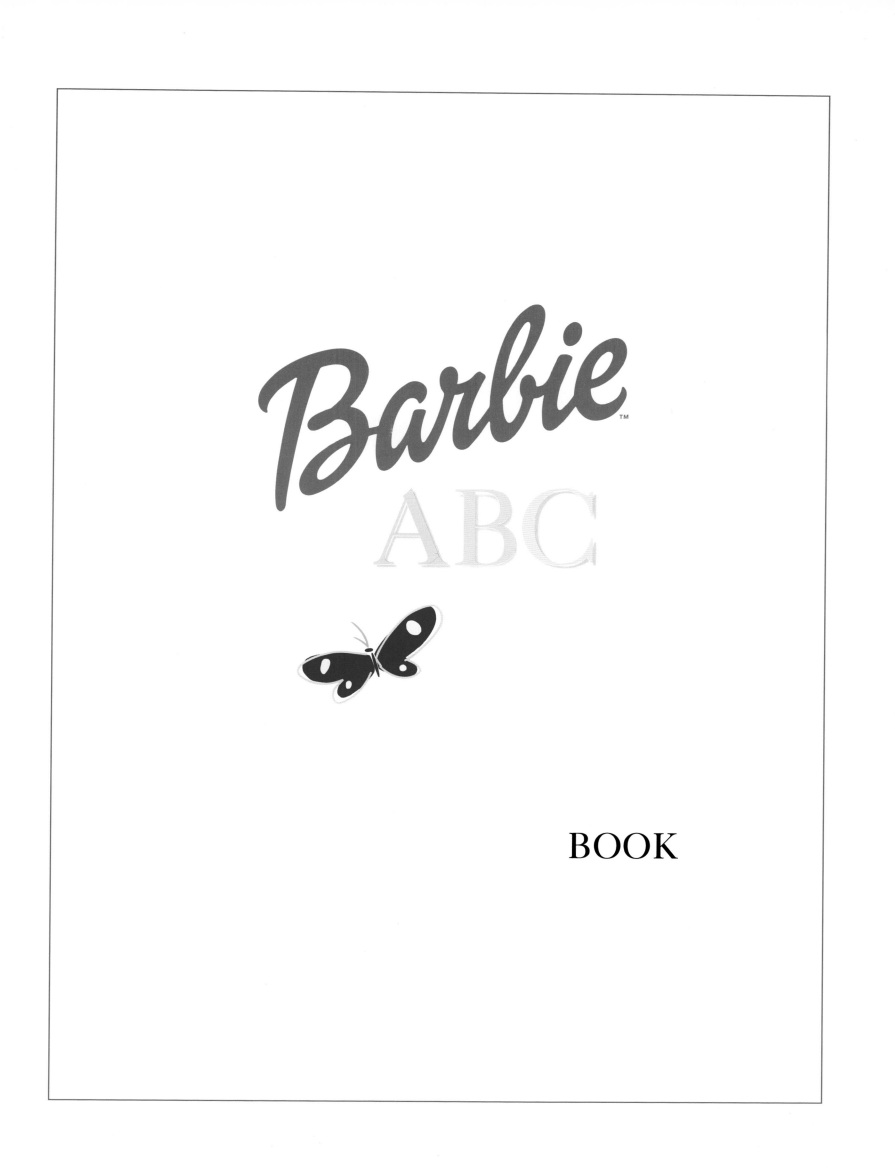

Barbie

ABC

BOOK

DK

Dorling Kindersley
LONDON, NEW YORK, SYDNEY, DELHI, PARIS,
MUNICH, AND JOHANNESBURG

Designed by Brian Voakes
Written by Rebecca Smith
Senior Editor Marie Greenwood
Managing Art Editor Jacquie Gulliver
Senior Managing Editor Karen Dolan
Production Joanne Rooke

Photography
Geoff Dann
(pages 4, 6, 10, 12, 14, 16, 18, 19, 21, 24, 27-29)
Mattel photography by Scott Fujikawa, Susan Kurtz, Dave Bateman,
Steve Alfano, and Judy Tsuno

Published in the United States by
Dorling Kindersley Publishing, Inc.
95 Madison Avenue
New York, New York 10016

First American Edition, 2000
2 4 6 8 10 9 7 5 3 1

BARBIE and associated trademarks are owned by
and used under license from Mattel, Inc.
Copyright © 2000 Mattel, Inc. All Rights Reserved.

All rights reserved under International and Pan-American Copyright Conventions. No part of this
publication may be reproduced, stored in a retrieval system, or transmitted in any form or by any
means, electronic, mechanical, photocopying, recording, or otherwise, without the prior written
permission of the copyright owner. Published in Great Britain by Dorling Kindersley Limited.

Color reproduction by Media Development, UK
Printed in
L.E.G.O., Italy.

BARBIE -- the abc book -- 1st American ed.
p.cm.
Summary: Each letter of the alphabet is represented by photographs of Barbie accompanied by puzzles to
solve and objects to find.
ISBN 0-7894-5334-7
[1.Dolls--Fiction. 2. Alphabet. 3. Picture puzzles.] I. DK Publishing, Inc.

PZ7 .B23343 2000
[E]--dc21

About this book:
There is a complete word list at the back of this book containing
every alphabet object found in the pictures.

For our complete catalog visit
www.dk.com

Barbie

ABC

BOOK

A Dorling Kindersley Book

Find an alligator, an astronaut, and an alien.

Admire the adventurous armadillo and point to the anchor.

A a Look at the amazing array of artwork in this art gallery.

Can you see an airplane, and some apples and an avocado? Spot the ankles.

Count the arrows and the angels.

I'm at the ballet in a box with my boyfriend Ken.

Find the birds, the boat, and the bouquet on stage.

Can you see my bracelet, brooch, bouquet, and bright blue bag?

Bb

I am wearing a ball gown. Can you see Ken's bow tie?

Cc

Look at all the colorful things I have collected on my checkered cloth.

Point to the cat on a chair and the caterpillar in a corner.

I'm dancing at a disco, wearing my new dress!

Dd

Look at the dots on my dress and count the dramatic discs on the floor.

Can you find a dozen doughnuts and a dozen drinks? Find the drums!

Point to the disco ball and find some diamond shapes.

Find an explorer near an elephant on an escalator!

Ee

I am eager to examine this extraordinary Egyptian scene.

An eagle exists above an elk. Find an envelope and a ewe. Spy an eye and an ear!

Look at the exercise bike next to the eclipse. Find an elbow and an emerald.

In the evening the empress examines her egg timer.

Here I am in my fabulous fairytale world.

My fortress is flying five flags and is surrounded by fir trees and forests.

Find the frog and four forks. Count the fresh flowers and the four fawns.

Ff

Do you like my favorite fluffy feather fan?

Glance at the goose with a golden egg and the grapes.

Gg

Gaze at the G words in my gold and glittering fairy castle.

Look at the green grass and count the glass objects. Can you find the gloves?

Gaze at the gentle green giraffe and the gorgeous gems on the gold goblet.

Guess how many gold coins are gathered by the goblet.

Hello! Here we are on a hilltop with our horses.

Someone has a hat in her hand, an H on her horse, and a hair band on her head.

How many hats can you see? Look at the hedges.

Count the horses' hooves, and find two hearts.

I i

Imagine how very icy it is inside this incredible icebox.

How interesting to find three isolated ice-cream sundaes inside!

Inquire about how many icicles are hanging in front of the ivy.

Indicate where the I on the igloo is.

I have journeyed to the jungle with Ken.

J j

I am wearing jeans and a jacket. Can you see seven jugs?

Look at the jade jewelry. Ken is jotting down his thoughts in a journal.

Watch out for the jaguar in the jungle! Find the hidden J.

Count the knitting needles on the K page.

K k

I want to keep all these kittens. I will kiss them and be kind to them!

Kittens keep knocking knitting yarn into knots all over the kitchen!

Keep track of the kittens making knots with the knitting yarn.

Do you know how many keys are kept on this K page?

I love making lemonade for lunch.

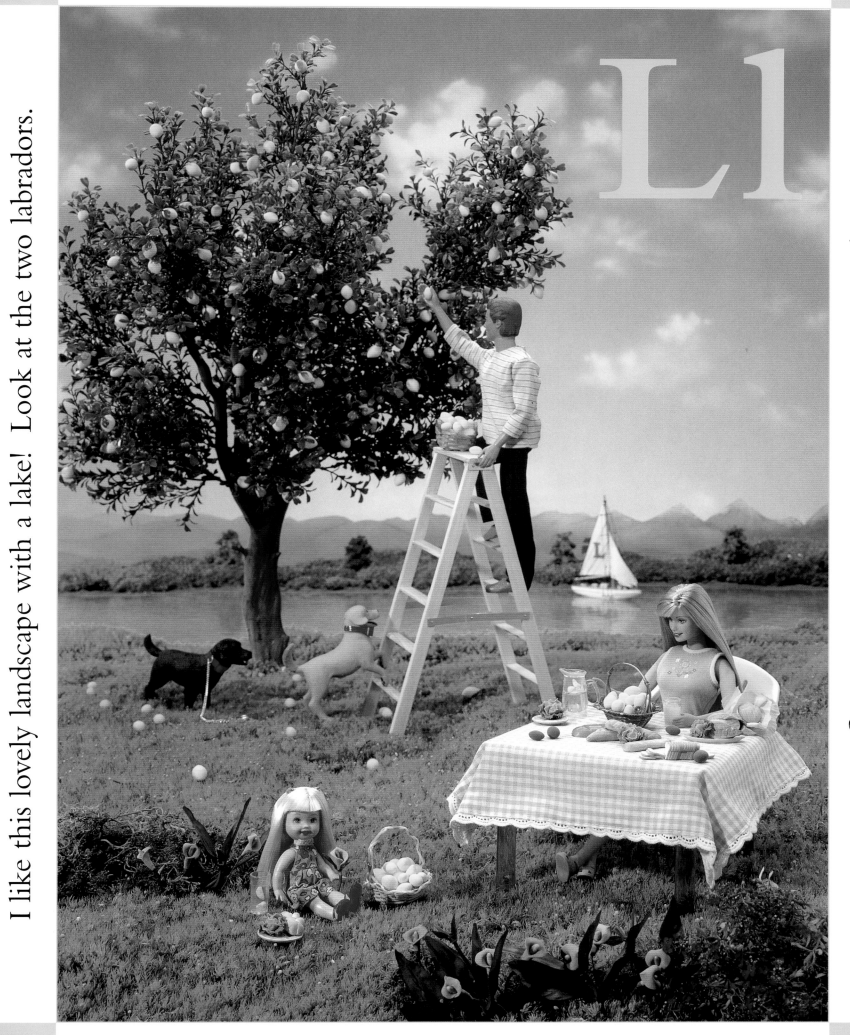

I like this lovely landscape with a lake! Look at the two labradors.

How many limes are on the table? Who is leaning on the ladder?

Count the loaves of bread, heads of lettuce, and the lilies.

Marvel at this model's messy makeup desk.

A model's life is full of makeup!

Mm

I must mention the mauve makeup and the mystery mouse!

Find a measuring tape, a mug, and two mascara brushes.

It is nighttime and I'm writing in a notebook.

Nn

Can you see my new night-light, a newspaper, and nine nail polish bottles?

Have you noticed my necklaces, the sewing needles, and the number nine?

Look at the nightingale. Count my nighties. Find the N.

Out in the ocean can you observe four oars?

Oo

Oh! Look at that smiling orange octopus on the ocean wave.

Where is the lifesaving O shape in the ocean? Find two oranges!

Can you find the number one, the old owl, and the odd ostrich?

The octopus has offered to help the orangutan.

Pink and purple look perfect in this playroom.

Count the pots of paint, pencils, puppies, and potato-shaped Ps on paper.

Point out three parrots, a puppet, three penguins, a pelican, and two pigs.

Where is a puzzle of a pony? Point to the panda bears.

I love to imagine myself as a queen.

Qq

It is quaint to be queen of hearts in this imaginary world.

How many question marks can you see? Look at the quiche and the quilt.

A queen must have a quill to write down her questions.

In this quiet garden there are several quails.

Look at the range of colors in this real rose R.

Count the red rings and the red roses. Look at the ribbon behind the R!

Count the rabbits playing with the roses. How many roses are there in the R?

Remember to record how many rings you can see.

I am standing in the sunshine with Stacie.

S s

It is summertime and the sun is shining on the sand. I want to go swimming and splash around in the sea!

Can you find a sailboat on the sea, a seagull in the sky, and seven sandcastles?

Spot my snorkel, a stereo, a seal, and some stray starfish on the sand.

Stare at my shiny surfboard and smile when you see an S.

It is time for tea at the tennis tournament.

Spot a telephone and two trophies on the table. Now try to find the tiny turtle.

Count three slices of toast. Can you find thirteen tennis balls? Look at the trees!

There are three trucks, two trains, one tie, and ten tulips.

These umbrellas are blowing up and down.

U u

Look at my unusual friend floating in my favorite umbrella!

How many umbrellas can you see? How many are upside down?

This unicorn finds his upturned umbrella very useful.

Can you see the U shapes on the umbrella handles?

I am on the veranda of my villa looking at the view.

The violet flowers are very beautiful – they also match my outfit!

Can you see a vast volcano, a village, and a valley?

Count the vases. Look at the violin and the vines.

Ww

This week we are walking in the woods with our waterproof jackets on.

Can you see a wicker basket, three wheels, some water bottles and a waterfall?

The weather is windy but we are warm because we are wearing our woolen hats.

Find the wheelbarrow, a watermelon, and a woodpecker.

Examine this extraordinary X page.

X x

Can you imagine an X-ray of a xylophone?

It is extremely exciting to play music on your own xylophone.

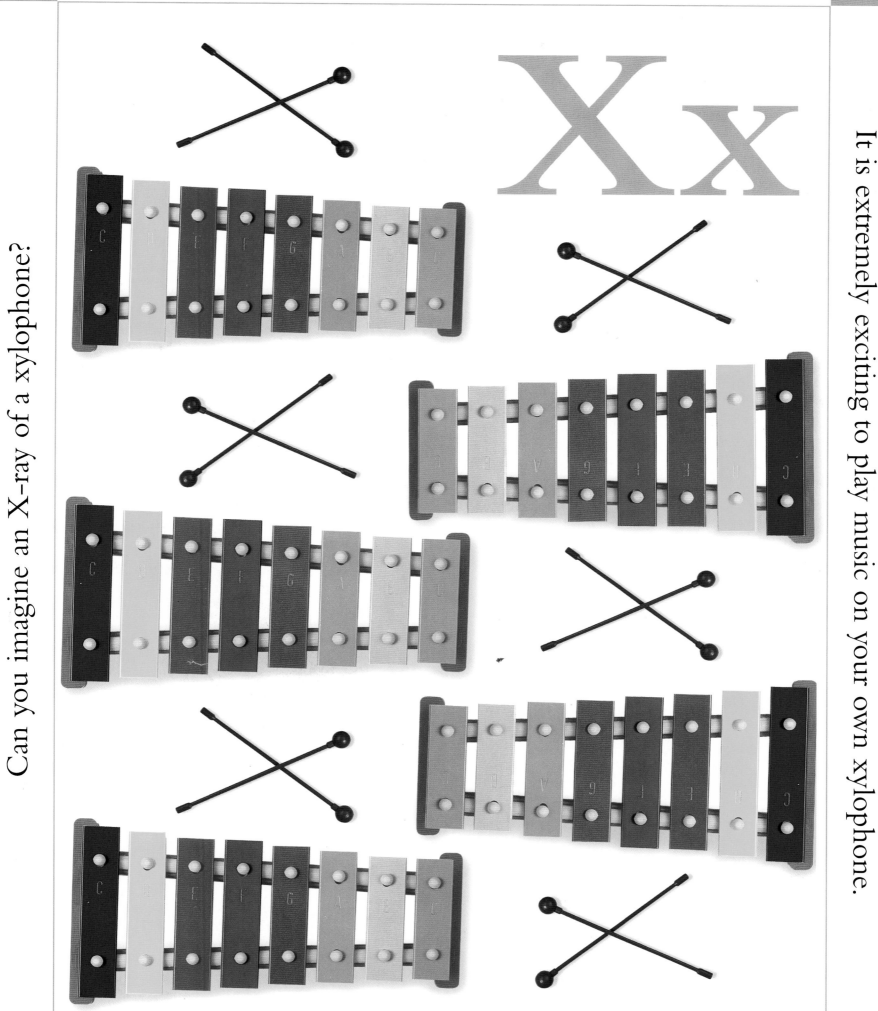

Count the extra Xs and the xylophones.

Yy

Yippee! I love
yellow yo-yos!

Yawn when you see a yellow pepper! Can you see a yellow sun?

Yell "yes" when you spot the yellow yolk! Can you see a Y?

y

Yodel when you see two yachts! Count the smiling yo-yos.

Y

It is almost time to zip up this Z page.

The zebra that escaped from the zoo is ready to go to sleep ... "zzzzzz...."

Zoom around the Z page to count the Zs and the zippers!

The zippers make a zigzag shape like a Z.

WORD LIST

Here is a list of the alphabet objects that appear in this book. Can you read the words then find the objects?

A

airplane
alien
alligator
anchor
angels
ankles
apples
armadillo
arrows
astronaut
avocado

B

bag
ball gown
ballerina
Barbie
binoculars
birds
boat
bouquet
bow tie
box
bracelet
brooch

C

cake
camel
candle
car
carrots
cats
caterpillar
chair
checks
chocolate
clock
cloth
clown
coins
comb
cow
crowns

D

diamond shapes
disco ball
discs
dots
doughnuts
drawstring slacks
dress
drinks
drums

E

eagle
ear
earring
eclipse
egg
egg timer
Egyptian
elbow
elephant
elk
emerald
empress
envelope
equal sign
escalator
ewe
exercise bike
explorer
eye
eyebrow

F

fan
fawns
feather
feet
fir trees
flags
flowers
forest
fork
fortress
frog
fruit

G

gems
giraffe
glass
gloves
goblet
gold coins
goose
grapes
grass

H

hair
hair band
halter
hand
handkerchief
hats
head
hearts
hedges
hilltop
hooves
horses

I

ice
ice cube
icebox
ice-cream sundaes
icicles
igloo
insects
ivy

J

jacket
jade
jaguar
jeans
jewelry
journal
jugs
jungle

K

keys
kittens
knitting yarn

L

labradors
lace
ladder
lake
leash
leaves
lemons
lemonade
lemons
lettuces
lilies
limes
loaves

M

makeup
mascara brushes
measuring tape
mini skirts
mirror
model
mouse
mug

N

nail polish
necklace
needle
newspaper
night-light
nighties
nightingale
notebook
notes

O

oars
ocean
octopus
oranges
orangutan
ostrich
owl

P

paint
panda bears
paper
parrots
pelican
pencils
penguins
pens
pictures
pigs
polar bear
pony
potato
pots
puppet
puppies
puzzle

Q

quails
queen
question marks
quiche
quill
quilt

R

rabbits
ribbon
rings
roses

S

sailboat
sand
sandcastles
sandals
sea
seagull
seal
sky
snorkel
spade
Stacie
starfish
stereo
sun
sunglasses
sun-hat
surfboard

T

table
tea
teacup
teapot
telephone
tennis balls
tie
toast
trains
trees
trophy
trucks
tulips
turtle

U

umbrellas
unicorn

V

valley
vases
veranda
villa
village
vines
violet flowers
violin
volcano

W

water bottles
waterfall
watermelon
waterproof jackets
wheels
wheelbarrow
wicker basket
woodpecker
woods
woolen hats

X

xylophone

Y

yachts
yellow pepper
yolk
yo-yos

Z

zebra
zigzag shape
zippers